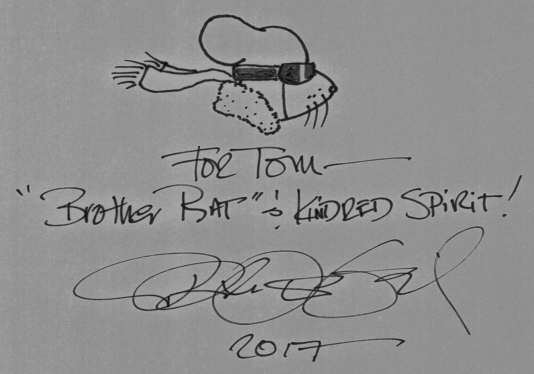

For Tom—
"Brother Bat"! Kindred Spirit!

2017

MOTOMICE

Art and Words by Paul Owen Lewis

 BEYOND WORDS
Hillsboro, Oregon

Everyone knows what **BIKERS** are like.

Bikers wear **BLACK**. They look **TOUGH**.

Their motorcycles are **LOUD**.

Bikers wear ORANGE. They look like PILOTS.

Their motorcycles are OLD.

Bikers wear PINK. They look like RACERS.

Their motorcycles are FAST.

Bikers wear YELLOW. They are GRANDMAS and GRANDPAS.

Their motorcycles CARRY EVERYTHING.

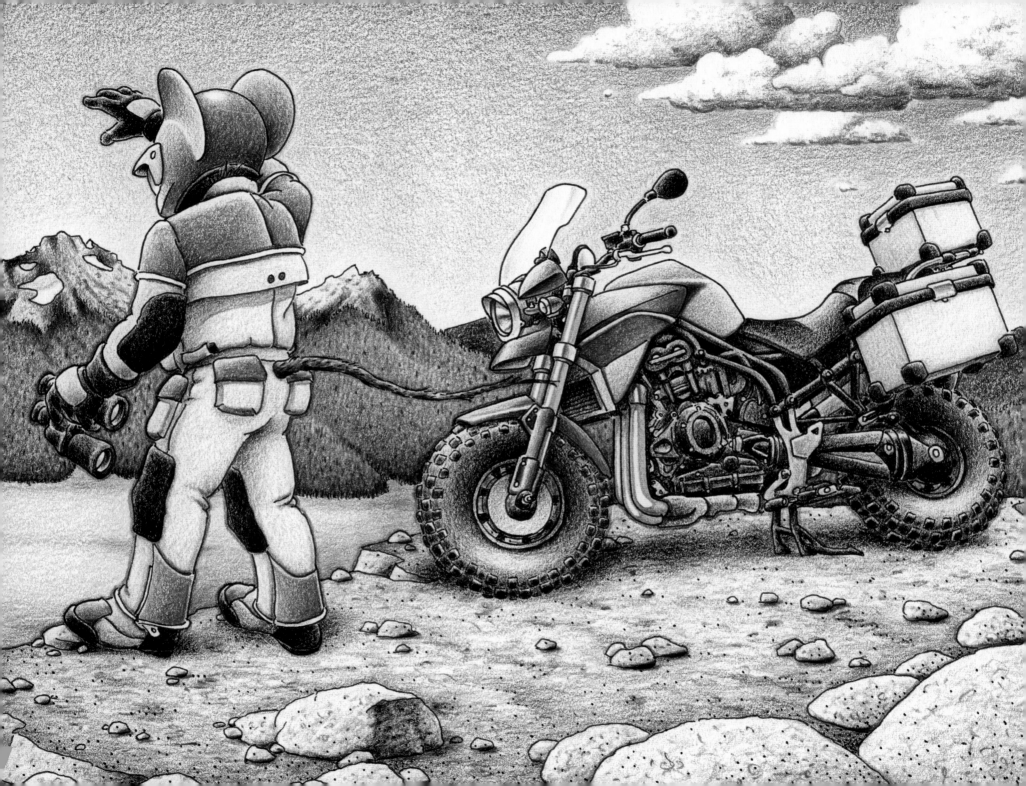

Bikers wear BLUE. They look like ASTRONAUTS.

Their motorcycles GO ANYWHERE.

Bikers wear **GREEN**. They care about the **ENVIRONMENT**.

Their motorcycles are **QUIET**.

BIKERS ARE every color, every style,

and **EVERY KIND OF PERSON.**

BIKERS ARE like FAMILY.

Everyone knows what BIKERS ARE like.

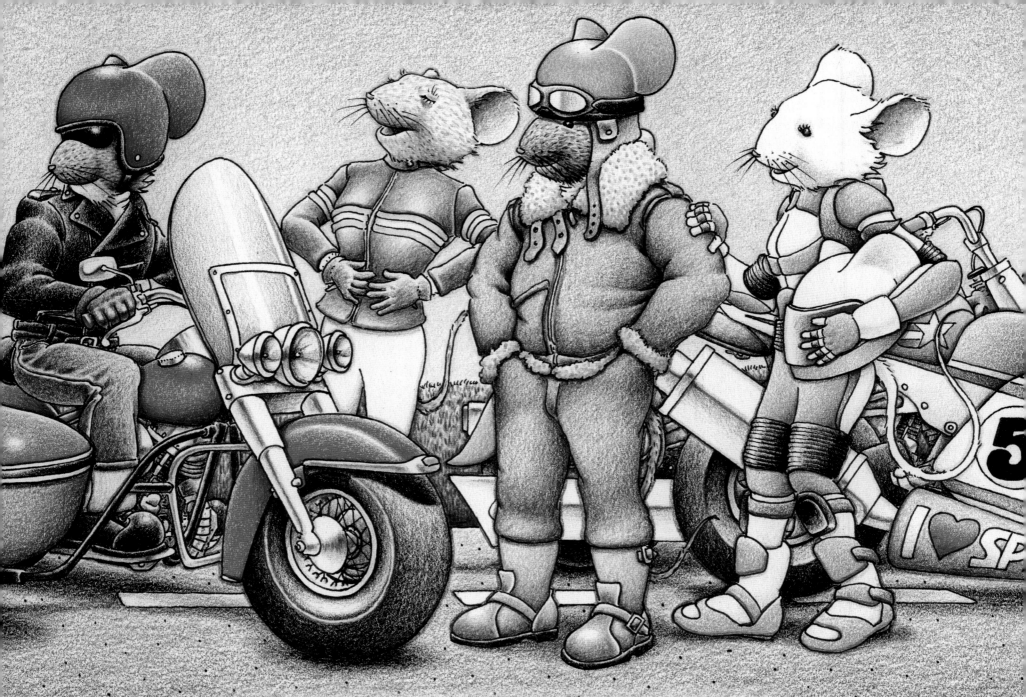

They are JUST LIKE YOU AND ME.

For David,
My brother in life and on the road.

SEMPER FI

The artist has made his best efforts to create symbolic representations of various motorcycle genres or types in common use today. Any resemblance to an actual manufacturer's motorcycle model is purely coincidental.

BEYOND WORDS

20827 N.W. Cornell Road, Suite 500
Hillsboro, Oregon 97124–9808
503–531–8700 / 503–531–8773 fax
www.beyondword.com

Design: Lorna Nakell

First Beyond Words hardcover edition May 2017

Beyond Words Publishing is an imprint of Simon & Schuster, Inc. and the Beyond Words logo is a registered trademark of Beyond Words Publishing, Inc.

For more information about special discounts for bulk purchases, please contact Beyond Words Special Sales at 503–531–8700 or specialsales@beyondword.com.

Manufactured in Korea

10 9 8 7 6 5 4 3 2 1

Library of Congress Control Number: 2017933593

ISBN 978–1–58270–660–3

The corporate mission of Beyond Words Publishing, Inc.: Inspire to Integrity